To Ralston and Reagan,
Joshua and Jacob.
Stewart, thanks for your support.
— M.R.

I Love the Skin I'm In
Text copyright © 2012 by Mayma Raphael
Illustrations by Haily Cryan
Illustrations copyright © 2012 by Mom Publishing

Library of Congress Control Number: 2012902325

ISBN: 978-1-795-15168-9
First Edition — 2012 / Designed by Rebecca A. Stone
Published by Mom Publishing
2625 Middlefield Rd. Palo Alto, CA 94306
www.mompublishing.com

I Love the Skin I'm In!

By Mayma Raphael • Illustrated by Haily Cryan

PUBLISHING

"Mommy, why is my skin brown?" Ruby asked her mother while they were at the playground.

"Ruby, my dear,
  you were created like this,"
  Her mother replied
  and gave her a kiss.

"Did you know
  that your skin makes you unique?
  Just like your great smile
  and the way that you speak.

How amazing it is that the skin that you're in
Can often tell a lot about your kin.

OUR

It may let people know who your ancestors are
And whether they came from near or from far.

WORLD

Your beautiful brown skin
will always be with you
Even as you grow older,
becoming whatever you want to."

Ruby grew excited about the things she could be
And happily shared them with her mommy,

"I can be a teacher,

a mother,

a president,

or a lawyer

an astronaut,

a dancer,

a princess,

or a doctor!"

Ruby paused and wondered, "Why do my friends have skin colors that are different?"
Her mother answered as Ruby kept silent.

"The color of their skin is only on the outside
As everyone is the same on the inside

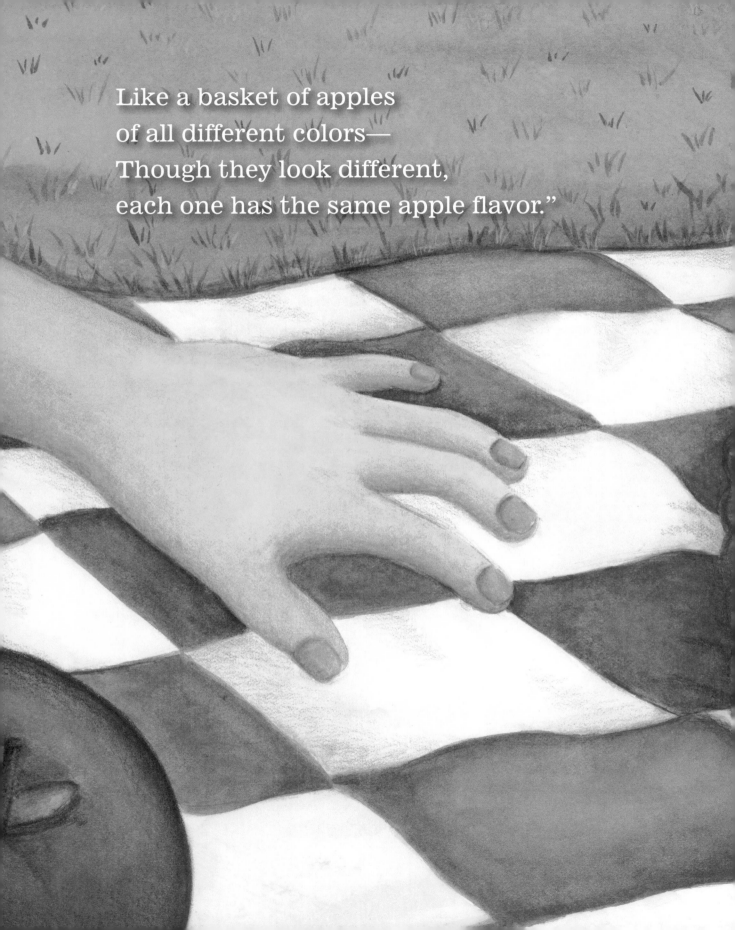

Like a basket of apples
of all different colors—
Though they look different,
each one has the same apple flavor."

Ruby, now pointing to her friends,
asked her mother,
"Mommy, is one skin color
much nicer than another?"

Her mother responded
with a smile on her face
As Ruby smiled back
and they warmly embraced,

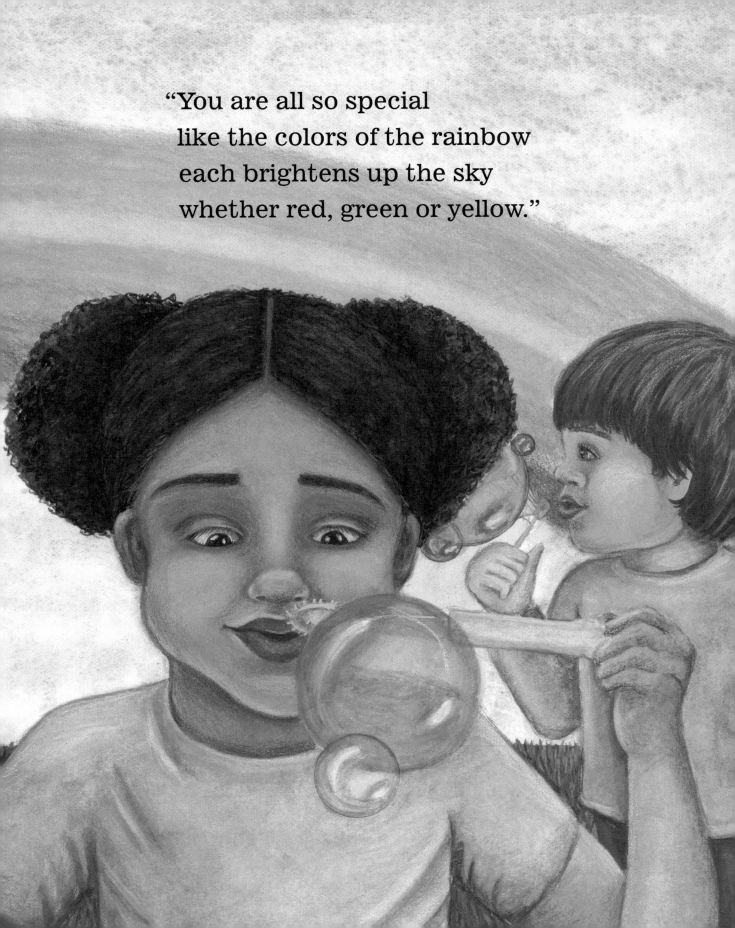

"You are all so special
   like the colors of the rainbow
   each brightens up the sky
   whether red, green or yellow."

Ruby smiled from ear to ear
Her mother's words she was happy to hear.

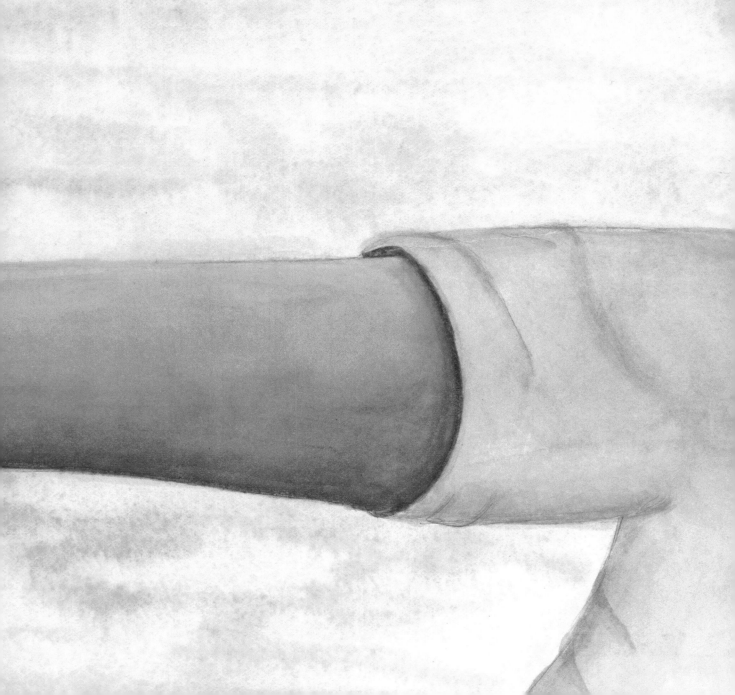

And she then yelled,
with that very same grin,
"Mommy, I really do love
the skin I'm in!"

Made in United States
Troutdale, OR
09/12/2023

12844218R00019